FOR SUMMER AND DANNY

Gary The GoatMoosse

by Nicholas Cull

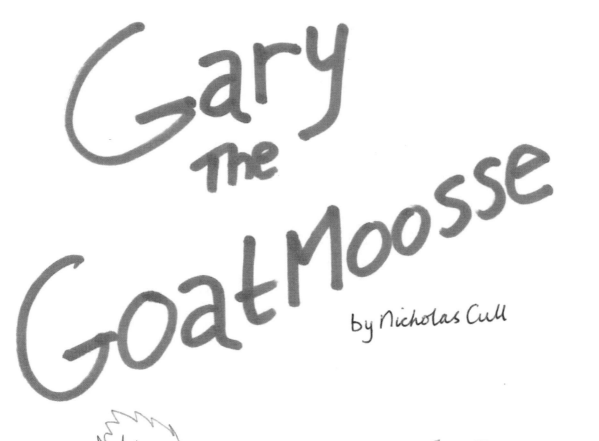

Being Di... K... is OK

BEING DIFFERENT is OK

BEING DIFFEREN

is OK BEING DIFFEREN

is OK BEING DIFFEREN

is OK BEING DIFF is OK

Being DIFFR NT is OK

BEING DIFF R NT is OK

BEING DIFRNT is OK

PEING DIFFRNT

Hi, I'm Gary the Goat Moose

I live in the northern hemisphere where the grass meets the snow and the flat land meets the mountains

My mum was a high mountain moose and my old dad was a rufty tufty billy goat. Anyway, they fell in love and that is how I became a goat moose.

As my old dad used to say 'you should never judge a goat by its cover' or something like that. But it can still be tough being a goat moose sometimes.

I simply don't seem to fit in with all the other animals. They look at me in a strange way and don't know what sort of animal I am.

So one day I decided to
head out into the world
to see if I could meet
other animals that
looked like me.

I kissed my mum and
dad goodbye and set off
towards the hidden
valley, where I knew
there was plenty of food
and water.

It was a beautiful sunny day as I trotted along the path, whistling as I went. As I trotted I realised I was being followed.

I was quite scared at first, but I stayed on the path towards the hidden valley and kept whistling to myself.

Even though I was scared, I overcame my fears by singing songs and telling myself stories. I started to realise I am quite a good story teller and before I knew it I had arrived at the hidden valley.

As I munched away on some juicy leaves I heard a rustle behind me.

It startled me so much I jumped in the air with fright.

Is it a Mountain Lion?!

Could it be a Tiger?!

To my surprise a very large red and black striped frog type animal hopped out from behind the hedge

"Hello", he said, "I'm Terry."
"Hello", I said, "I'm Gary."

"Iv'e been following you", said Terry.
"I'm a bit lost and very lonely."
"You gave me quite a fright", I said, "but that's OK."

"What sort of animal are you?" I asked.
"I'm a Tiger Toad", said Terry.
"That's great", I said, "I'm a Goat Moose."

Terry told me he was very sad
because he didn't seem to fit
in with all the other animals

So the two of us stayed in the valley eating leaves and telling our stories to each other. We were so happy that time flew by until it started to get dark.

As it was getting dark Terry asked:
"I suppose I should be on my way now?"
I thought about it for a split second and said, "Of course not Terry. Although we look different, we have so much in common and we are similar in many ways. I have found someone that I am happy to be different with. Being different is OK. If we stay together we will be safer and much happier."

Terry agreed and so we cuddled
together under a big oak tree
and told each other stories
under the stars until we fell asleep.

THE END

BEING DIFFERENT IS OK

BEING DIFFERENT IS OK

BEING DIFFERENT

BEING DIFFERENT

IS OK BEING DIFFERENT

IS OK BEING DIFFERENT

BEING DIFFERENT IS

BEING DIFFERENT IS

BEING DIFFERENT IS

BEING DIFFERENT IS

BEING DIFFRENT

BEING DIFFERENT IS OK!

BEING DIFFERENT IS OK!

BEING DIFFERENT

EING DIFFERENT

EING DIFFERE

S OK! BEING DIFFER

BEING DIFFEREN

ING DIFF RATIS O

EING DIFFR ATIS

BEING DIFFR ATIS

BEING DIFFRENT

BEINY DIFFRATIS

GoodBye for now!

Goat Moose is different
Goat Moose is kind
He traveled a long distance
to see what he could find
Hello Tiger Toad you're different like me
Let's play together 'til the end of the day
Goat Moose is different but that's OK
Goat Moose, Goat Moose
Hip Hip Hooray!

Printed in Great Britain
by Amazon